A Day
of
Surprises

by Sylvia Root Tester
illustrated by Frances Hook

THE
CHILD'S
WORLD

ELGIN, ILLINOIS 60120

Library of Congress Cataloging in Publication Data

Tester, Sylvia Root
  A day of surprises.

  SUMMARY: Saralinda's day is full of surprises
which the reader is asked to identify and remember.
  I. Hook, Frances. II. Title.
PZ7.T288Day   [E]   78-23263
ISBN 0-89565-022-3

A Day
of
Surprises

"I have a surprise to show you," Daddy said. He took Saralinda outside to the tree. He lifted her high on his shoulder.

"Oh!" she said. "Oh my! One, two, three, four of them!"

Her daddy set her down again.

"Was that a good surprise?" he asked.

"That was a great surprise!" she said.

(What was the surprise?)

Then Daddy and Saralinda took a walk. She held onto three fingers of his hand. She always did that, because his hand was so big.

"Look!" she said. "Another surprise!"

"How about that!" said her father. "And right on the sidewalk too! Let's help it get to the grass."

Ever so gently, Daddy picked it up and placed it in the grass.

(What was the surprise?)

The next surprise, Saralinda found all by herself. She was smelling some honeysuckle.

"Uh-oh!" she said. She stood very still. Then she moved backward...carefully...very carefully. Then she ran all the way into the house.

"Some surprises aren't so nice!" she told her mother.

(What was the surprise?)

"I know a better surprise," said her mother. "It's waiting for you over at Tanya's house."

"I'll bet I know! I'll bet I know! Is it..."

"Run over and see," said her mother. "But come right back."

Saralinda ran to Tanya's house. Sure enough! Just as she thought! There were...

(What was the surprise?)

Saralinda and Tanya petted the kittens. Oh, they were careful! They used only one finger each, because the kittens were so tiny.

Then Saralinda remembered. "I have to go right back home," she said.

On the way, she saw some pretty pink petunias. She stooped down to look at them.

"Oh!" she said. "Another surprise! There on the flower!"

(What did she see?)

"Uncle Gregory is coming for lunch," said Mother, as Saralinda came in the door.

"He is? Is he riding..."

"I think so."

Soon Uncle Gregory arrived. "I have a surprise for you," he said to Saralinda. He held it behind his back.

"Let me see! Let me see!"

But when she looked around one way, he turned. And when she looked around the other way, he turned again.

(What was the surprise?)

Finally, he showed it to her.

Saralinda laughed. "Just my size!" she said.

"And..." said Uncle Gregory, "if your mother doesn't mind, there's another surprise."

Mother smiled and nodded.

So Saralinda and her Uncle Gregory went outside.

(What did they do?)

They rode on his motorcycle... all the way around the block! Saralinda laughed and laughed and waved at everyone she saw.

At lunch, there were no surprises. But after lunch...well! Uncle Gregory ran out to his motorcycle and ran back in. He had a box. He let Saralinda smell the box.

"I know!" she said. "I know! It's..."

"Don't tell!" he said. "Don't spoil the surprise!"

Then he opened the box.

(What was inside?)

"It's nap time," said Mom.

"I'm not sleepy," said Saralinda.

"Rest anyway," said Mom. So Saralinda lay down in the bed. While she rested, she made her own surprise. She took something tiny and wrapped it in half a tissue. Then she put it in a little box.

"Surprise!" she said to Mom when naptime was over.

"Oh, what a lovely surprise!" said her mother. "And it fits so nicely! How did you think of it?"

(What did Saralinda put in the box?)

Daddy came home early. "Hurry!" he called. "Get ready! We'll be late!"

"Where are we going?" asked Saralinda. Daddy grinned. "You'll see."

Uncle Gregory grinned. "I'll never tell!"

Mommy grinned. "It's a surprise."

All of them piled into the car. They drove and drove and drove. And then they were there.

"I know! I know!" said Saralinda. "We're at..."

(Where were they?)

Grandma hugged Saralinda, and Grandpa hugged Saralinda. And everyone talked at once.

Saralinda waited. She tried to be patient. She waited a long, long time.

Finally, she couldn't wait any longer. She took Grandpa's hand. She tugged and tugged.

Grandpa looked down and grinned.

"Ready?" he asked. He always had a surprise for her.

"Yes! Yes! Yes!" she said.

"Look in my sweater pocket."

(What was the surprise?)

"You know what?" Saralinda said. She blew some bubbles.

"What?" asked Grandpa.

"I've had a whole day of surprises! A whole wonderful day!"

(Can you remember all of Saralinda's
surprises?)

About the Artist

Frances Hook was educated at the Pennsylvania Museum School of Art in Philadelphia, Pennsylvania. She and her husband, Richard Hook, worked together as a free-lance art team for many years, until his death. Within the past 15 years, Mrs. Hook has moved more and more into the field of book illustrating.

Mrs. Hook has a unique ability for capturing the moods and emotions of children. She has this to say about her work. "Over the years, I have centered my attention on children. I've done many portraits of children. I use children in the neighborhood for my models. I never use professional models."

A great admirer of Mary Cassatt, an American Impressionist, Mrs. Hook enjoys doing fine art as well as commercial work.

About the Author

Sylvia Root Tester has been writing for children for twenty years. She has written fairy tales, folk tales, fantasy, science fiction and real-life stories, as well as supplemental teaching books. In addition, she has written works for teachers and for parents. As her own children were growing up, she tried out her stories on them. Now she uses nephews and nieces as her sounding board.

"I enjoy writing for children," she says. "If I can spark a child's imagination, or if I can make a child say, 'Yes, that's the way it is,' I've done my job."